Grandmother
Ptarmigan

Grandmother
Ptarmigan

by Qaunaq Mikkigak and Joanne Schwartz
illustrated by Qin Leng

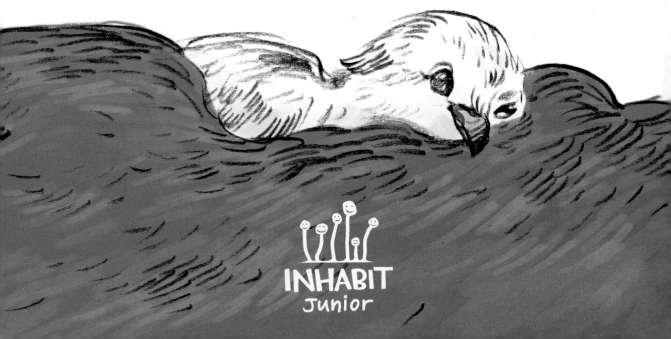

INHABIT
junior

Once there was a little ptarmigan who
would not go to sleep.
His grandma sang him a lullaby. But he
would not go to sleep.
His grandma said, "Close your eyes now."
Still he would not go to sleep.

The little ptarmigan said, "Grandma, tell me a story."

And Grandma said, "I don't have a story to tell. Tuck in and go to sleep."

He said, "Grandma, tell me a story."

And Grandma said, "I don't have a story to tell. Tuck in and go to sleep."

Again he said," Grandma, please tell me a story!"

And so, Grandma told her little ptarmigan a story,
a story so he would stop asking.

"See, over there in the porch, there are baby
lemmings with no hair.
They want to come over
here and get warm."

The little ptarmigan started to
squirm.

"They want to crawl up your back,
under your armpits,
around your neck.
They want to crawl inside."

The little ptarmigan squirmed even more.

"Oh no, here they come!"
And with that, Grandma tickled her little
ptarmigan here, there, and everywhere.

The little ptarmigan shook, shook with fright!
And then that little ptarmigan, who had never
flown before, jumped up and flew away.

"Oh, my poor, frightened little grandson has flown away," Grandma cried. "Nauk, nauk."
"Where did he go, where did he go?" Grandma cried. "Nauk, nauk."
"Oh, my poor, frightened little grandson has flown away. Nauk, nauk, nauk."

Once there was a little ptarmigan who would not
go to sleep.
And that is why baby ptarmigans fly so young.
And that is why female ptarmigans cry nauk, nauk.

Qaunaq Mikkigak is an elder, artist, and throat singer from Cape Dorset, Nunavut. She was born in 1932 in the Cape Dorset area and grew up on the land in a traditional Inuit community. She was featured in the books *Inuit Women Artists: Voices from Cape Dorset* and *Cape Dorset Sculpture*. In 2011 she collaborated with author Joanne Schwartz on a picture-book version of the traditional Inuit tale *The Legend of the Fog*. She is well known locally for her storytelling, and her throat singing has been featured on several recordings.

Joanne Schwartz was born in Cape Breton, Nova Scotia. She has been a children's librarian in Toronto, Ontario, for over twenty years. Joanne has written articles for *Canadian Children's Book News* and other publications. Her picture books include *Our Corner Grocery Store*, *City Alphabet*, and *City Numbers*. In 2011 she collaborated with Inuit elder Qaunaq Mikkigak on a picture-book version of the Inuit tale *The Legend of the Fog*. *Our Corner Grocery Store* was nominated for the 2010 Marilyn Baillie Picture Book Award. She lives in Toronto with her two daughters.

Qin Leng was born in Shanghai and has lived in France and Montreal. She now lives and works as a designer and illustrator in Toronto. Her father, an artist himself, was a great influence on her. She grew up surrounded by paintings, and it became second nature for her to express herself through art. She graduated from the Mel Hoppenheim School of Cinema and has received many awards for her animated short films and artwork. Qin Leng has always loved to illustrate the innocence of children and has developed a passion for children's books. She has published numerous picture books in Canada, the United States, and South Korea.

Published by Inhabit Media Inc. • www.inhabitmedia.com

Inhabit Media Inc. (Iqaluit), P.O. Box 11125, Iqaluit, Nunavut, X0A 1H0
(Toronto), 146A Orchard View Blvd., Toronto, Ontario, M4R 1C3

Editors: Neil Chirstopher and Kelly Ward
Art director: Danny Christopher

We acknowledge the support of the Canada Council for the Arts for our publishing program.

Printed and bound in Hong Kong by Paramount Printing Co. • August 2013 • #135814

Canada Council   Conseil des Arts
for the Arts   du Canada

Library and Archives Canada Cataloguing in Publication

Mikkigak, Qaunak, author
        Grandmother ptarmigan / written by Qaunaq Mikkigak and Joanne
Schwartz ; illustrated by Qin Leng.

ISBN 978-1-927095-52-2 (bound)

        I. Schwartz, Joanne (Joanne F.), 1960-, author II. Leng, Qin, illustrator
III. Title.

PS8626.I4196G73 2013   jC813'.6   C2013-903148-0

INHABIT
Junior